A Good Team

Read more UNICORN and YETI books!

UNICORN and YETI

A Good Team

written by
Heather Ayris Burnell

art by
Hazel Quintanilla

ACORN™
SCHOLASTIC INC.

For Elijah. So glad you're on my team! — HAB

To my dad, who teaches me to find happiness every day in everything — HQ

Library of Congress Cataloging-in-Publication Data

Names: Burnell, Heather Ayris, author. | Quintanilla, Hazel, 1982-illustrator.
Title: A good team / by Heather Ayris Burnell ; illustrated by Hazel Quintanilla.
Description: First edition. | New York, NY : Acorn/Scholastic Inc., 2019. |
Series: Unicorn and Yeti ; 2 | Summary: New friends Unicorn and Yeti are having a little trouble finding something they are both good at; Yeti is good at kicking a ball, Unicorn is not, Unicorn is fast, Yeti is not—so they finally try ice skating, which neither of them has ever done, because they have a chance to be equally good (or bad) at it.
Identifiers: LCCN 2018035382 | ISBN 9781338329049 (pbk.) | ISBN 9781338329056 (hardcover)
Subjects: LCSH: Unicorns—Juvenile fiction. | Yeti—Juvenile fiction. |
Ability—Juvenile fiction. | Friendship—Juvenile fiction. | Humorous stories. | CYAC: Unicorns—Fiction. | Yeti—Fiction. | Ability—Fiction. | Friendship—Fiction. | Humorous stories. | LCGFT: Humorous fiction.
Classification: LCC PZ7.B92855 Go 2019 | DDC [E]—dc23 LC record available at https://lccn.loc.gov/2018035382

10 9 8 7 6 5 4 3 2 1   19 20 21 22 23

Printed in China 62
First edition, July 2019

Edited by Katie Carella
Book design by Sarah Dvojack

Table of Contents

The Ball

Unicorn saw Yeti kick the ball.

That looks fun!

I like to kick the ball.

You are good at that.

I like to bounce the ball on my knee.

You are good at that too.

4

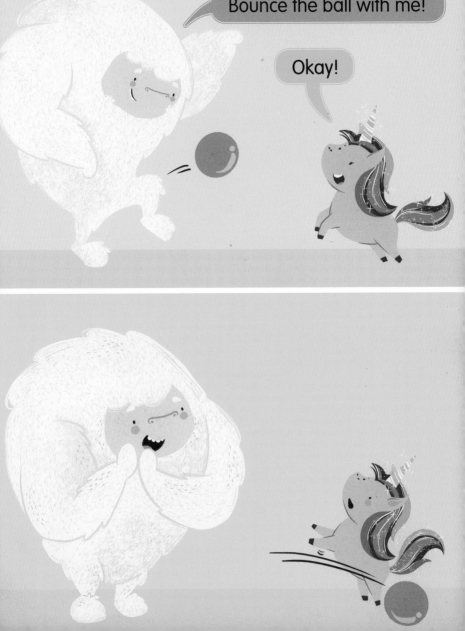

I am not good at bouncing the ball on my knee.
The ball did not even touch your knee.

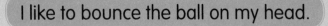

I like to bounce the ball on my head.

You are very good at that!

Bounce the ball with me!

Okay!

7

Look!
The ball is
on my head!

I am **so** good at
bouncing the ball on my head
that it did not come off.

8

You did not bounce the ball on your head.
The ball is **stuck** on your head!

9

You look funny with the ball stuck on your head.

I feel funny with the ball stuck on my head.

Oh no!

I cannot get the ball off my head.

11

Now the ball has a hole in it.
It is not a ball anymore.

No it is not.

It is a ring!

How are we going to play together now?

You cannot kick the ring with me. You cannot bounce the ring with me.

That is true.

14

But I bet you will be very good at **tossing** the ring.

You want me to toss the ring?

Yes! Toss the ring to me.

15

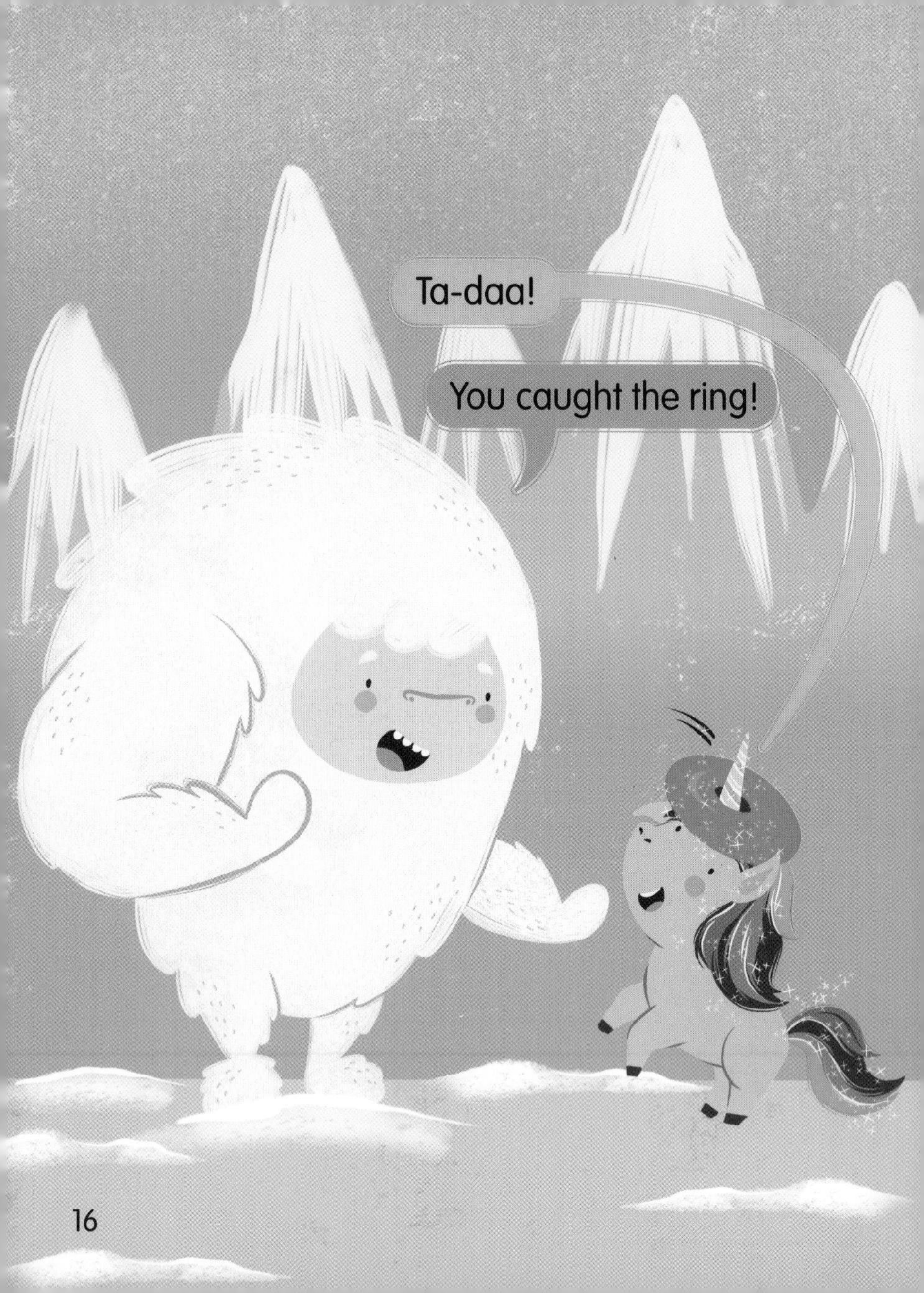
Ta-daa!
You caught the ring!

Unicorn and Yeti played ring toss again . . .

and again . . .

and again!

You are good at catching the ring!

It helps that I have a horn.
Plus, you are very good at tossing the ring!

19

A Race

Let's have a race.

What kind of race?

A running race!

Running is not fun.

Running is the best!

What kind of race do **you** think would be fun?

A rock-moving race would be fun.
HAHA!
HEHE!
A rock-moving race sounds hard.

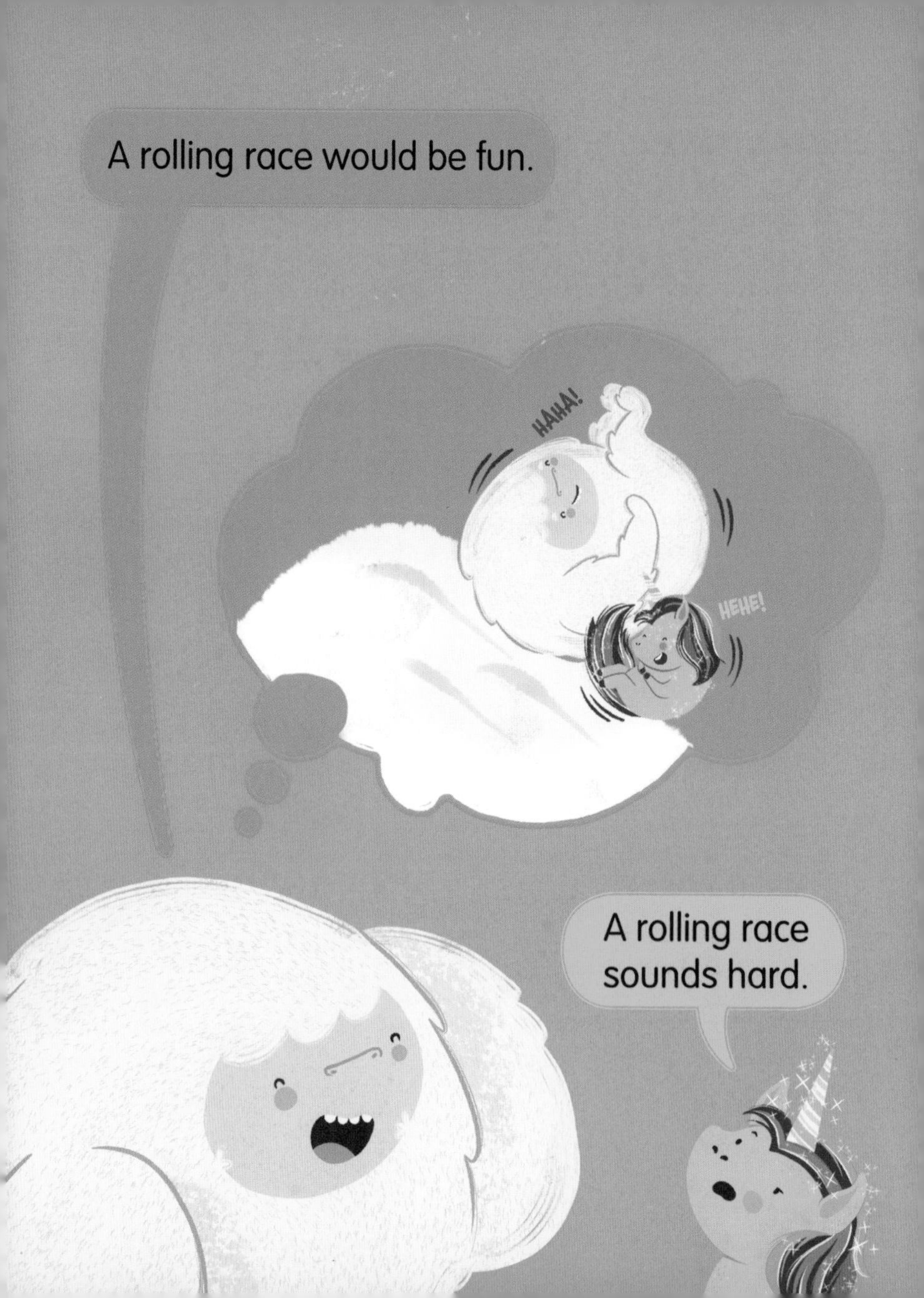
A rolling race would be fun.
HAHA!
HEHE!
A rolling race sounds hard.

A roaring race would be the best.

ROAR!

ROAR!

Roaring is not a race.

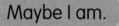

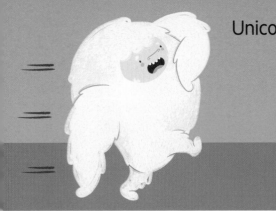

Unicorn and Yeti ran.

Yeti kept running.

Then Yeti saw a rock!

29

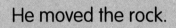

He moved the rock.

Yeti kept running.

Then Yeti tripped!

He rolled.

He roared.

Yeti kept running.

34

You made it!

I am not a fast runner.

That is okay.
The race was just for fun.
Did you have fun?

I did not think
a running race
would be fun.
But it was.

Let's have another race!

Another **running** race?

A rock-moving, rolling, roaring, running race!

That sounds hard. I am not sure I know how to have that kind of race.

I will help you. It will be fun!

We will be a racing team!

Ready. Set. Go team!

37

On Ice

Look! Ice!

We should stay away from it.
We could slip and fall.

Ice **is** slippery.
That is what makes it fun.
We should skate on it.

I cannot ice skate. I do not know **how** to ice skate.
I do not know how to ice skate either.

We might be bad at ice skating.

Or we might be good at ice skating.

We will not know unless we try!

First, we need ice skates.

I like these ice skates!

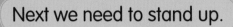 Next we need to stand up.

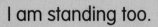 I am standing.

I am standing too.

44

45

Look at me!
I am ice skating!

I can skate forward.

I can skate backward.

46

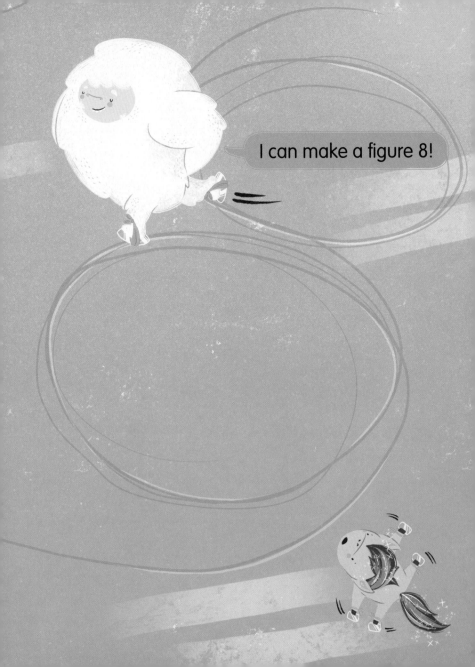

You are a natural!

You are not a natural.

48

49

Stand up.

Stand all the way up!

Now slide one foot.

Now slide the other foot.

We can dip.

We can twirl.

We are a
good team.

I am ice skating!

I am glad we tried to skate, even though ice is slippery.

Ice skating feels magical!

Ice skating makes me thirsty. Let's get some hot cocoa.

With rainbow sprinkles.

Hot cocoa and sprinkles are the perfect pair.

Just like us!

56

About the Creators

Heather Ayris Burnell lives in Washington state where she loves to ice skate. Sometimes she even has hot cocoa with sprinkles afterward. Heather is a librarian and the author of *Kick! Jump! Chop! The Adventures of the Ninjabread Man*. Unicorn and Yeti is her first early reader series.

Hazel Quintanilla lives in Guatemala. Hazel always knew she wanted to be an artist. When she was a kid, she carried a pencil and a notebook everywhere.

Hazel illustrates children's books, magazines, and games! And she has a secret: Unicorn and Yeti remind Hazel of her sister and brother. Her siblings are silly, funny, and quirky — just like Unicorn and Yeti!

YOU CAN DRAW YETI!

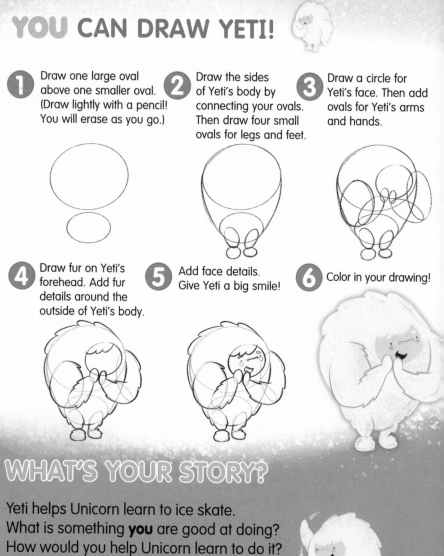

1 Draw one large oval above one smaller oval. (Draw lightly with a pencil! You will erase as you go.)

2 Draw the sides of Yeti's body by connecting your ovals. Then draw four small ovals for legs and feet.

3 Draw a circle for Yeti's face. Then add ovals for Yeti's arms and hands.

4 Draw fur on Yeti's forehead. Add fur details around the outside of Yeti's body.

5 Add face details. Give Yeti a big smile!

6 Color in your drawing!

WHAT'S YOUR STORY?

Yeti helps Unicorn learn to ice skate.
What is something **you** are good at doing?
How would you help Unicorn learn to do it?
Write and draw your story.

scholastic.com/acorn